Dear Parents:

Congratulations! Your child is taking the first steps on an exciting journey. The destination? Independent reading!

STEP INTO READING® will help your child get there. The program offers five steps to reading success. Each step includes fun stories and colorful art or photographs. In addition to original fiction and books with favorite characters, there are Step into Reading Non-Fiction Readers, Phonics Readers and Boxed Sets, Sticker Readers, and Comic Readers—a complete literacy program with something to interest every child.

Learning to Read, Step by Step!

Ready to Read   Preschool–Kindergarten
• big type and easy words • rhyme and rhythm • picture clues
For children who know the alphabet and are eager to begin reading.

Reading with Help   Preschool–Grade 1
• basic vocabulary • short sentences • simple stories
For children who recognize familiar words and sound out new words with help.

Reading on Your Own   Grades 1–3
• engaging characters • easy-to-follow plots • popular topics
For children who are ready to read on their own.

Reading Paragraphs   Grades 2–3
• challenging vocabulary • short paragraphs • exciting stories
For newly independent readers who read simple sentences with confidence.

Ready for Chapters   Grades 2–4
• chapters • longer paragraphs • full-color art
For children who want to take the plunge into chapter books but still like colorful pictures.

STEP INTO READING® is designed to give every child a successful reading experience. The grade levels are only guides; children will progress through the steps at their own speed, developing confidence in their reading. The F&P Text Level on the back cover serves as another tool to help you choose the right book for your child.

Remember, a lifetime love of reading starts with a single step!

For school librarians everywhere
—S.L. & M.L.

Text copyright © 2006 by Sally Lucas.
Illustrations copyright © 2006 by Margeaux Lucas.

Visit us on the Web!
StepIntoReading.com
randomhousekids.com

Educators and librarians, for a variety of teaching tools, visit us at
RHTeachersLibrarians.com

Library of Congress Cataloging-in-Publication Data
Lucas, Sally.
Dancing dinos go to school / by Sally Lucas ; illustrated by Margeaux Lucas. — 1st ed.
    p.   cm. — (Step into reading. Step 1 book)
Summary: A surprised librarian and a young reader watch as dancing dinosaurs in a book leap
off the page and into the school, causing havoc in the classroom and on the playground.
ISBN 978-0-375-83241-3 (trade) — ISBN 978-0-375-93241-0 (lib. bdg.) —
ISBN 978-0-307-97887-5 (ebook)
[1. Dinosaurs—Fiction. 2. Schools—Fiction. 3. Stories in rhyme.] I. Lucas, Margeaux, ill.
II. Title. III. Series.
PZ8.3.L966Das 2005 [E]—dc22 2005011572

Printed in the United States of America
34 33 32 31 30 29 28

This book has been officially leveled by using the F&P Text Level Gradient™ Leveling System.

by Sally Lucas

illustrated by Margeaux Lucas

Random House 🏠 New York

Dinos dancing
in a book.

Dinos leaping,
look, look, look!

Dinos landing

on the floor.

Dinos dancing
more and more.

Dinos peeking
through the glass.

Dinos sneaking

into class.

Jiggling, wiggling
to and fro.

Wiping chalkboards
as they go.

Dinos reading ABC.

Dinos counting 1, 2, 3.

Dinos pasting
red and blue.

Dinos wasting
paint and glue.

Dinos taking

every snack.

Dinos putting
each one back.

Dinos running

out to play.

Dinos cheering

all the way.

Dinos jumping
hand in hand.

Dinos digging
in the sand.

Dinos soaring
on the swings.

Higher, higher—

School bell rings!

Stopping, dropping
very fast.

Chasing, racing

back at last.

Dinos leaping,
look, look, look.

Dinos dancing

in a book.